HAPPY TIMES

IN

CZECHOSLOVAKIA

DRAWINGS BY YARKA BURES

New York · ALFRED · A · KNOPF · London

1 9 4 0

HAPPY TIMES
IN
CZECHOSLOVAKIA

by LIBUSHKA BARTUSEK

Foreword by Eleanor Roosevelt

DEDICATED

TO MY MOTHER AND FATHER

MARIE & JAN BARTUSEK

AND MY FRIEND

MARIE BURÉS

✳

TO THEM AND TO ALL THOSE

OTHER COURAGEOUS SOULS

WHO SOUGHT

A NEW HORIZON

Foreword by Eleanor Roosevelt

AT THIS TIME *when the world is full of things which bring us sorrow, I think this little book should be an asset to our children's education. They will learn that Czechoslovakia, a small young democracy, was taken over by a totalitarian government. The new government may obliterate some of the things which have existed in this little country for some time; such as the background of national culture. Nothing is ever lost, however, as long as it lives in books and pictures and in the hearts of the children.*

This book is a cheerful and charming picture of the life and experiences of childhood in Czechoslovakia. It will influence the thought of our own children and perhaps be of value in making them cherish their own traditions.

I wish the authors of the text and of the drawings every success in the perpetuation of the things which they so evidently hold dear in their native land.

CONTENTS

The Awakening

*These are the names
of the people and things in this book, and this is how
they are pronounced:*

[a *as in* what; e *as in* get; i *as in* it; o *as in* or; u *as in* out]

Starechek, the grandfather	Sta'-reh-check
Starenka, the grandmother	Sta'-ren-ka
Tatichek, the father	Ta'-tyee-check
Mamichka, the mother	Ma'-mitch-ka
Tomash, the older son, eleven years old	To'-mahsh
Marushka, his seven-year-old sister	Ma'-roosh-ka
Yurka, their five-year-old brother	Your'-ka
Horak, their last name	Ho'-rahk
Anichka, the hired girl	A'-nyitch-ka
Stepan, the hired man	Shtyeh'-pahn
Yanko, the blacksmith	Yan'-ko
Vavrova, a neighbor	Vah'-vro-vah
Father Bohdan, the priest	Father Boh'-dan
Doubek, the baker	Dough'-beck
Skopek, the Horaks' uncle	Shko'-peck
Tetichka, their aunt	Teh'-tyitch-ka
Patek, the schoolmaster	Pah'-teck
Koshila, a shirt	ko'-shil-la
Galhoty, pants	gal'-ho-ty
Buchty, coffee-cakes	booh'-ty
Morana, straw-stuffed dummy, "Old Woman Winter"	Mo'-ra-na
Kolachky, little tarts	ko'-latch-ky
Aldamash, a bouquet-wreath	al'-da-mahsh

The Awakening

MARUSHKA opened one eye very carefully. It was a beautiful big brown eye and its twin was just as beautiful and big and brown when *it* was opened. She peered over the top of the puffy feather-bed as if she were looking over a haycock. What was to-day? Of course it was Sunday, but it was a special Sunday, one that was to be full of exciting happenings. For the first time in her whole life she was to be allowed to join her big brother Tomash and the other children of the village in celebrating the passing of winter.

> *Saint George comes,*
> *Takes out his keys,*
> *We know;*
> *Unlocks the earth*
> *That flowers and trees*
> *Might grow . . .*

. . . and Grandma, or 'Starenka' as they all called her, let her voice trail off into a thin, thready melody that Marushka loved to hear.

3

Marushka, Yurka and Tomash

"Tomash!" cried Marushka, looking towards the bed in the other corner of the room, "Tomash! It's to-day!"

"What's to-day?" droned a sleepy voice from beneath the feathery mound on the other gaily painted bed.

"It's Judica! . . . The day we throw Old Woman Winter into the brook."

"Ho! So it is!" and out leaped Tomash, looking very much like any other boy in the world ready to have a fine time. Into his koshila first, that was the shirt, embroidered at the front and shoulders; then into his Sunday galhoty, a fine pair of dark blue pants with black embroidery down the front of the legs, and last of all, black boots and a leather belt with brass nail-heads driven into it, to ornament it.

Marushka crept out gingerly from her high bed. It was March and still cold in the early morning. She slipped quickly into the chemise that was spread on a chair by her bed and then turned to the large basin of water that the hired-girl Anichka had prepared for her the night before. She washed very carefully, not missing either ear. When she had finished, she called Anichka, knowing that Mamichka would be extremely busy. Anichka hurt her when she combed her hair and mothers were always so gentle, but she must be brave and endure the pain of pulled hair, now that she was old enough to join the other big girls of the village in their fun.

"God give you a good morning, Marushka," said Anichka in her clear high voice. Marushka thought it sounded like the silvery bell in church. "And you too, Tomash."

"Thank you," answered both children.

Anichka had cheeks like two luscious red apples, and white, white teeth that gleamed like snow when she smiled. She also had two forget-me-not blue eyes that never missed a thing.

"Tomash, of course you are very big, now that you are eleven."

"You are quite right, Anichka."

"And very big boys do not need to be told about cleanliness."

Tomash bowed his head. He had wavy brown hair that grew quite long in front. It fell like a little curtain over the top of his face. He was thankful that Anichka and Marushka could not see him blush. His face was very hot, and he remembered how stupid Yanko, the young blacksmith, appeared when, as he looked at Anichka, his face turned as red as the field-poppies.

He unfastened the fine leather belt, pulled off his koshila and went to work on his face and neck, scrubbing twice as hard as usual. He would show the girls that he was not afraid of cold water!

"Children, children!" Mamichka's voice rang out from the combined sitting-and-dining-room, just as Marushka and Tomash entered very quietly. They were hungry, but they did not rush. Instead, they bowed,—first, to Starechek and Starenka (Grandfather and Grandmother), and then to Mamichka and Tatichek (Mother and Father). As they bowed low, they gravely said, "Praised be our Lord Jesus!"

Yurka, who was just five, and a year-and-a-half younger than Marushka, was already at the table. He looked so clean he fairly shone. He was very much the baby to the two older children; he still wore skirts! Not skirts exactly, but a shirt that hung loose and long like a skirt, and was beautifully embroidered at the front and shoulders, like Tatichek's and Tomash's. He even wore handsome boots like theirs, and his tiny sheepskin coat, with the fuzzy side turned in, and his warm astrakhan cap, hung side by side with those of the other men of the household.

Marushka was now fully dressed in a little white blouse, two starched petticoats and a finely pleated black skirt, the front of which was covered by a flowered silk apron. Lovely embroidered ribbons, tied about her waist, made her look just like

6

a flower garden. She looked exactly like Mamichka, only, of course, she was smaller.

The older members of the family were quite wide awake by this time. They had already attended church. They seated themselves at the table; Tatichek at the head, Mamichka at the foot. Starenka and Starechek with Tomash and Marushka were on one side; Anichka on the other, between Yurka and the hiredman, Stepan. They all bowed their heads solemnly as Tatichek thanked the good Lord for His bounty and asked His blessing on them all, family and servants alike.

The coffee was for the grown-ups only, for the children drank buttermilk; but the smiling buchty (little round coffee-cakes filled with cheese, prune-jam, or poppy-seed) were for them all, and no one had to be coaxed to eat!

Immediately after breakfast, Marushka tied her red kerchief on her head and put on her winter coat. It was of sheepskin too, only, instead of being brown as were the men's and older boys', hers was snow-white and wonderfully embroidered. Tomash handed her the tiny tree they had decorated with many-colored ribbons the day before. Holding the tree very tightly, so that it would not fall, she proudly set forth to meet the other girls in the village square.

When they had all gathered, they started out in a group, the oldest girl, Kachka, leading them. It was a very pretty picture, these eager, rosy-cheeked little girls, carrying be-ribboned trees, singing as they went from door to door in the village:

> *Saint George comes,*
> *Takes out his keys,*
> *We know;*
> *Unlocks the earth*
> *That flowers and trees*
> *Might grow.*

7

It was the same song that Starenka had sung so many, many years ago, and which she still sang when she thought of her childhood.

After the house-to-house procession, Marushka was joined by her brothers Tomash and Yurka. All the other boys, whether they had sisters or not, met the group, and then, one and all, they hurried on to church.

Marushka was a bit tired after tramping through the village. Her boots were heavy, but she was very brave. If she expected to take part with the others in the afternoon celebration, she must not give in. After all, she was six years old—in fact, six and one-half.

When the children returned to their white house with the brightly decorated entrance hall, Marushka was so excited, telling about the morning experiences, that she completely forgot about being tired. Mamichka, however, made them all keep very quiet for a while, and soon they were calm enough for their dinner.

There was noodle-soup, boiled beef, delightful, fluffy dumplings and horse-radish gravy. It was all so well-prepared that no one had time for talk. Besides, the children would not think of talking unless they were spoken to.

"We've made you a splendid Morana," said Tatichek to the children at the close of dinner. Tomash and Marushka were all smiles.

"May I have some too?" chirped Yurka, and everyone laughed, not harshly, but kindly.

"Morana is the pretend-figure of Old Woman Winter and all her ills," explained Tatichek. "Mamichka took some sack-cloth and made a fine-looking figure with legs, arms, and a head. Stepan is a real artist. He painted the face, and I stuffed the sack with straw. We all helped dress the Old Woman so that she looks quite human, hung high on her pole."

8

Holding the tree tightly, she set forth

By the time Tatichek had finished, Stepan was out in front of the house with the straw-stuffed dummy that was Morana. Tomash sped towards the door to accept his precious load.

"Tomash! Your coat!" Starenka called after him. It was strange how grandmothers always noticed things like that; wet boots, uncombed hair and going without one's coat when it was cold. He put on his sheepskin coat and thanked Starenka for reminding him.

The rest of the children were waiting at the statue of Saint John. When they saw the Horak children coming towards them, and Tomash carrying the figure of Morana on its tall pole, they all let out a cheer. Then, two by two, they followed him down to the brook, that was swollen with the melting of the mountain snows.

Tomash waited until all the children had reached the banks and then, with a sweeping gesture, he tossed Morana out into the middle of the stream. The figure was caught by the swift current and amid the happy cries of everyone, was carried on and on.

As one of the older girls started to chant, they turned to go back to the village, and soon everyone was singing:

> *Death is floating far away,*
> *Lovely spring is on its way.*

Spring Is Here

IT HAD BEEN a busy week. Everyone in the house helped in some way or other. Even little Yurka did his share, for on the Saturday before Floral Sunday, he and the hired-man Stepan had gone to gather pussy-willows.

"Really, Stepan," Yurka said, on their way back from the woods, "I feel much older than just five. Don't you think I am quite grown-up?"

"I was thinking *that* this morning," agreed Stepan. "It seems to me that you have grown at least two centimeters within the past month."

Yurka drew himself up to his full height. "Well," he sighed, "I shan't have to wear this silly shirt much longer. Tatichek promised to let me start school this coming Fall. Then I shall have trousers!"

Within a few steps of the parsonage towards which they were headed, they met the priest.

"Praised be our Lord Jesus!" said Yurka solemnly, as he took off his cap with his free hand, and bowed.

The kindly priest patted Yurka's blond little head and said,

11

Two by two they followed Tomash

"May our Lord bless you, my son. You must have been out early to have gathered such fine willow-cats. They are beautiful." Then, as Yurka smiled proudly, the good man added, "Would you like to carry them into the church for me?"

This was quite beyond Yurka's greatest hopes. He almost forgot to answer in his excitement. Stepan looked at him severely. Yurka caught his look. "To be sure," he cried eagerly, and then remembering his manners, he added hurriedly, "Father Bohdan."

The next morning, on their way home from church, the family carried home the blessed pussy-willows, just as in many other countries people bring home palm leaves.

"Yurka, what lovely branches you found!"

"Where did you get them?"

"Were they hard to cut?"

Questions and praise were heaped upon Yurka so generously, that his pride knew no bounds. Little as he was, he felt that at last he had taken his place in the big people's world.

Holy Week was to be a very busy one for the Horak family, for beside the religious services in which all shared, there were many preparations to be made for the festive celebrations which were to begin on Easter Monday.

From Monday through Wednesday everyone, particularly the older girls, painted beautiful Easter-eggs. That meant a great deal of work, because they were not painted in one color or simply dipped in a dye like most American Easter-eggs, but some of them took hours, and even a whole day to paint. They looked as though the tiny designs had been done with a pin-point.

There was no school for the children after Wednesday, but there was so much to do, that no one ever missed it. First of all, everyone went to church on Green Thursday. Then four times that day, at sunrise, at noon, at three o'clock, and again at sundown, all the school children formed in procession and marched solemnly through the village, calling out the hour. The girls wore head-kerchiefs, but the boys were bare-headed. Each one carried or pushed an odd noise-maker, which he twirled or shook with all his might, to make it rattle. This rattling took the place of the ringing of church-bells, which were always silenced on Green Thursday and Good Friday.

The Horak children went to bed early that night, but did not undress before lying down. They had one more duty to perform. At midnight, they were to celebrate the solemn rites of the "Washing of the Feet," a ceremony in which everyone, both old and young, took part.

And so, when Mamichka's gentle voice called them, they were ready.

"I know it is hard to waken in the middle of the night, but it is time to go," said she, quietly urging the sleepy children to hurry.

Tomash jumped up. He was rather surprised to find himself fully dressed. Then he remembered. "Marushka, we're going to the brook to wash our feet. Are you coming with us?"

By that time Marushka was wide awake. "Of course I am! Do you think I am a baby?"

Although it was still quite cold outdoors, particularly at midnight, everyone, young and old alike, walked barefoot to the little chattering brook. Here they all stepped into the cold waters and washed their feet. Marushka shivered the tiniest bit, as her toes touched the water, but Starenka, who always had a good reason for doing things, held her hand and declared, "That will make you healthy the rest of the year."

As they started back to the house, Marushka noticed that Anichka was carrying a pitcher of brook-water back with her. "Neighbor Vavrova is too sick to come out to-night, so I am taking the water to her and shall wash her feet," Anichka explained.

"It is too bad that she should not be able to share these rites with us."

"That is as it should be," said Starechek. "To serve is to live."

As Anichka hurried on to perform her task, the Horak family walked on slowly to their garden. It was a moonlit night and the delicate tracery of the early budding trees against the sky made Marushka feel as though she were in an unreal world. But soon the smell of the sweet earth reached her and made her want to kneel on the ground and touch it; touch it and thank it for being there.

The moment Anichka returned, Tatichek knelt, facing the East. The others followed his example, and there, in the stillness of the night, they prayed, remembering another prayer that had been offered in the Garden of Gethsemane many hundreds of years before.

The next day, Good Friday, was even more solemnly spent than the day before. There were the devotions in church and only the noon meal was served. Though the children repeated the calling of the hours with their noise-makers, they spoke very little. In fact they had been warned, days before, not to talk any more than was absolutely necessary. Even little Yurka remembered not to ask too many questions.

However, the pealing of bells early the next morning began that sunny day joyously. It was White Saturday. First came the lighting of the eternal fire in the churchyard and the blessing of the water for the baptismal font. Then, there were all the preparations to be made for Easter Sunday.

"May I help with the kolachky, Mamichka?" asked Marushka, when the family started the regular tasks after the morning services.

"I am baking a buchta, little daughter. It must be taken to church tomorrow to be blessed, along with the eggs. However, you may help Anichka with the sweeping and dusting. There must be no work on Easter Sunday."

After the sweeping and dusting, there were all the new clothes to be laid out for the children. At sundown the Resurrection services were held at which the children wore their very best clothes. Then all the new clothes for the grown-ups had to be laid out, for on Easter Sunday no one would think of wearing old clothes.

The day flew by as if it had wings, because everyone had so much to do. By the time Marushka, Tomash, and Yurka hung their little coats on the pegs in the living-room that night, three pairs of tired, tired eyes could hardly find the way to the bedroom.

Tired as they had been the night before, it was not very hard to get up the next morning. It was Easter, and Easter was such a joyous day! Perhaps it was because they all went to church together on this day that it seemed a particularly pleasant one.

They went to church without any breakfast, but on their return home, each member of the family ate one of the Easter-eggs that had been blessed.

"Now save the egg-shells," Starenka reminded them. "We'll crush them into little bits and carry them out to the fields. You know, scattering them there will make the soil rich and fertile." So the balance of the day was spent in sprinkling the fields with bits of egg-shell and visiting with kindly neighbors.

"Early to bed to-night, if you want to enjoy the Easter Monday chase," said Mamichka. The children needed no second invitation. The Easter chase was the high-light of the holidays, as far as the young people were concerned, and to miss it would be too bad.

Easter Monday was almost like St. Valentine's Day in other countries, only instead of giving valentines, Easter eggs were used. Among the older girls and boys it was quite a serious mat-

Spring is here

ter, for a girl would not think of giving up Easter-eggs to a young man whom she really did not like. However, among the children the chase was just a game.

All the boys made little switches of eight thin willow-shoots braided together. At the end of the switch was a bright red ribbon. With this in hand, they set out to chase the girls. Each girl had the lovely Easter-eggs she had painted wrapped in a red kerchief. And now the fun began. The boys started to chase the girls, trying to whip them with the little switches. The belief was that they were whipping them so that no dust would gather on them, but Starenka said, "It's to whip the demons out of the girls!"

At the end of the chase each girl gave the treasured eggs to one of the boys. The boy took the eggs out of the kerchief and tucked the kerchief into his boot-top. This meant that he liked that particular girl very much. Then he tossed the little switch up on the thatched roof of one of the houses so that the dust, accumulated on the switch, would not fall on anyone.

Tomash rushed into the house at noon, quite breathless and very red. He had been allowed to join the older group of school children, though Marushka and Yurka had not. "See here!" he cried, "I have had luck!" and he set down a basket of brilliantly decorated eggs.

"Mamichka, he has seven eggs in his basket, and all of them are beautiful!"

"Don't break them, Marushka. They were hard to get!" he warned his little sister.

"Oh, I'll be careful. I saw how hard you worked chasing the girls. Why do you chase so many, Tomash? The big boys only chase one girl." Marushka was really puzzled.

"Perhaps Tomash is just a bit greedy," reasoned Starenka, and then added, with a twinkle in her eye, "But it's just as well. There's safety in numbers."

"Well, this afternoon, we're to have more fun," Tomash went on, not quite understanding what Starenka meant. "The girls will chase the boys and try to get the eggs back. But the big boys have a plan."

"What is it? What is it?" cried Marushka and Yurka excitedly. After all, it was almost as good as actually being there, if one could be let in on a secret.

"Perhaps I shouldn't tell you. But I'm sure you won't tell." Then, assured by the honesty of their big round eyes, he continued, "Well, the boys are going to put up a scarecrow in the field, and then, when the girls chase them, they'll head for the field. That will end the game, of course. No girl would ever face the scarecrow. Not even to get an Easter-egg!"

"Goodness me!" sighed Mamichka at the end of the day, as she carefully folded away the Easter garments. "It was almost like Christmas, there was so much excitement." And then Mamichka turned to Anichka, who was arranging the first violets of the year in a gaily painted pottery jug. "Put the sheepskin coats in the big chest tonight, Anichka. Spring is here."

He leaned against the door

The Little Goose-Herd

"VERY WELL, Yurka, you say that you are a big boy. I shall give you something to do."

Yurka looked up at his father, hardly believing what he heard.

"The new little geese are to be taken to the meadow for the first time today. Do you think you can take care of them?"

Yurka's eyes were as large as tea-cups. He could not believe that all at once, he was to be given such a task.

"There are twelve of them, as you know. They are tiny goslings now, but I expect them to become very fine, fat geese. Of course, it will take both patience and time before we can roast one of them for a holiday dinner. Do you think you are equal to the work?"

"Oh yes, Tatichek, yes indeed! When shall I start?"

"You will start now. Stepan will lead you to the meadow and will come for you before noon."

Mamichka kissed Yurka's curly head tenderly as he started off for his first day's work. Surely, he had to grow up sometime, but it seemed such a short while ago that he was wrapped in a pillow, securely bound by banding, so that his little legs and back would grow straight and strong.

As Yurka and Stepan walked through the village, chasing the mother-goose and her little baby-geese before them, Yurka was certain that everyone was seeing them, particularly him.

It was a warm day, so that he was happy when they finally reached the fresh green pasture-land, where the geese would be satisfied to nibble at the new grass and not want to run in all directions.

Stepan left Yurka, after giving him final instructions. Suddenly the world seemed much larger than it had ever seemed before. The field flowers were just starting to show off their colored bonnets and the far-off hills were greener than they had been for months.

The mother-goose was kind to keep her babies so close to her. This was not going to be such hard work after all. Yurka pulled off his boots and wiggled his toes. The grass tickled his bare feet. He rolled over on his stomach, pulled out a blade of grass and started to nibble on it. It had a sweet flavor, almost like fresh young lettuce. No wonder the geese liked it. He liked it too. Why did grown-ups call them 'stupid geese'? He turned over on his sturdy little back.

A low rumbling noise wakened him. Where was he? In the meadow, of course. Where were the geese? There they were, still nibbling. There was a flash of lightning and then a clap of thunder. Yurka was not a coward; he was not afraid of storms. But the mother-goose started to honk in her funny voice and flap her wings, and the goslings were growing a little jumpy, as though they were afraid.

Where was Stepan? Surely it must be almost night-time, it was getting so dark. However, as long as there was no Stepan in sight, something must be done. Perhaps, if he could catch the mother-goose, the little ones would follow! But the mother-goose would not allow herself to be caught.

Yurka thought quickly. If he caught the goslings, the mother-goose would follow.

It was easy enough to catch the babies, and as he caught each one, he slipped it into his boot. At last he had them all, six in each boot, twelve all together. The mother-goose honked at him harder than ever. He paid no attention to her. He had to beat that thunder-storm home. So he ran as fast as he could, with the angry goose chasing him.

The house was very quiet when he entered. They were all still in the fields. It was storming now, but Yurka was safely within the door and the goslings were safe with him. He reached into one boot and drew out a limp little creature. Yurka turned very cold. The gosling was dead. He hastily drew out another. It was dead. One after the other. They were all dead, suffocated!

What would Tatichek say? What would Mamichka say? It had been such a joy and help to have twelve goslings that would some day soon become twelve fine fat geese! Yurka was beside himself. He could not face the disappointed look in Mamichka's face. He would rather be dead. Dead? That was it! Maybe if he were dead, they would not think of the geese so much, they would think more about him. He buried his head in his arms, leaning against the door.

"Yurka, what has happened?" It was Mamichka's sweet voice. Yurka sobbed as though his heard would break. He could not answer, he could only point with one hand to the stricken goslings.

"Yurka . . . Yurka! What have you done?" But the mute evidence showed Mamickha better than any words could have done. "Come! This is no time to cry. Get the large pillow off your bed and put it on the oven." Yurka obeyed. "Now put more wood into the stove." Again Yurka did as he was told.

23

Mamichka picked up the baby-geese, one by one, as though they were tiny babies, breathed on them as though she were breathing life itself into them, and then slipped each of the twelve under the pillow on the warm oven.

Then Mamichka and Yurka watched.

It seemed ages to Yurka, but really it was after a very few moments of expert treatment by Mamichka that the goslings started to stir. Yurka's eyes sought the blue of the sky, through the window. "Thank you, God, for letting them live."

The Ride of the Kings

WHAT EXCITEMENT there was in the village! Twenty of the finest youths between the ages of twenty-one and twenty-four had gone through the streets snapping long leather whips, until they cracked like fire-crackers. Marushka said whip-cracking reminded her of lightning, it was so sharp and clear. It would surely cleanse the place of evil spirits, just as Starenka said, and help prepare them all for Whitsuntide.

All the houses were decorated with linden boughs on Whit-sunday. This custom Starenka explained every year, so that the children might not forget it. "When Christ returned to meet with the Apostles, His enemies decided to mark the meeting-place with a bough of linden. But when His friends found out about the scheme, they all set branches of linden in front of their houses and in this way confused His enemies."

It was a beautiful day, all blue and gold, and the linden-tree under which they were sitting was so heavily fragrant, that Marushka could scarcely keep her eyes open. Of course, she had really no intention of falling asleep as it was only two in the afternoon, and she and Yurka had been allowed to walk down to the brook's edge, where the bluest and loveliest forget-me-nots grew like a carpet.

"A person hardly knows where the water stops and the for-get-me-nots begin," thought Marushka, as she pushed up her puffed sleeves so as not to get them damp, and stooped to pick the flowers. It was the first day of the year on which the girls in the village were wearing their huge white sleeves, that looked as though they were blown up by a bicycle-pump. They were so hard to keep fresh-looking, that Marushka was careful not to crush them. Mamichka had taken so much time putting in the hundreds of pleats.

"Tomash is very lucky, isn't he?" piped up Yurka as he trudged along at Marushka's side, carrying the sky-blue flowers.

"Why do you say that, little brother?"

"To think he is to be King . . ." went on Yurka, thinking out loud and not even realizing that Marushka was there. . . . "Per-haps I can be King too, when I am eleven. . . ."

"And why not?" Marushka interrupted him.

"Do you think I might?" and without waiting for Marushka's reply . . . "Just imagine . . . riding Tatichek's fine white horse, all decked out in ribbons, bells and flowers, with forty other boys around me on horseback."

"With your hands tied to the saddle, don't forget."

"Oh, I could do that!" boasted five-year-old Yurka.

"And you must wear a girl's dress, with a crown of ribbon streamers that flutter over your eyes. . . ."

"I wouldn't mind *that* for just once!"

"And carry a rose in your mouth all the while you ride, for you mustn't speak!"

Yurka was silent for a moment. "That would be hard, I think," he finally admitted.

Everyone was up bright and early Monday morning to see Tomash in the crown and dress, tied to Tatichek's snow-white horse. Two other boys, on horseback too, were the King's pages. There was one on each side, guiding the white horse, as they left the village for the meadow outside, where the forty riders on gaily bedecked horses were awaiting their King.

Now the game started. Stepan and Yanko, the two swiftest riders in the group, tore into the village like an arrow. They rode up to Tatichek's house first. Tatichek was mayor of the village and the riders had to have his permission to enter. The Horak family pretended they knew nothing of the game, but when it was carefully explained to Tatichek that the riders meant no harm, but simply wanted to collect food and money for the poor, he gladly welcomed them to the village.

Stepan and Yanko rode back to the group outside the limits, and soon the glorious procession of riders entered the village-green. The center section, including the King, pages, and twenty guards, marched in great style; the others carried huge baskets and rode a little apart. Then, as the King and his guard

Marushka

stood in the center of the green, certain chosen riders would approach a dwelling, stop in front of it and sing:

Heelom, heelom, high or low,
Landlord, farmer, as you go,
Listen well, that you may know
What this Whitsuntide doth blow.

Here before the house of Doubek
Doth my steed bow low his head
For he knows our happy baker
Bakes the finest kind of bread.

Needless to say, a pretty compliment such as this was well rewarded. Baker Doubek, his wife, and two buxom daughters, brought out loaves and loaves of bread. These were put into the baskets for the poor and the singing riders turned their horses to the next house. Here their fine singing brought money. Not much, to be sure, because the family was not so able to give, but the few coins were as graciously received as though hundreds had been given.

By the time the rounds of the village had been made, the baskets were overflowing; eggs, bacon, grain, and money. These were divided among the less fortunate, those whose crops had not yielded well the year before, or those who had so many children they could not feed or clothe them.

Now that their good deed was done, the boys returned their horses to the stables. Suddenly the village was alive with the noise of music—a thrilling march played by musicians, stationed in front of the inn. The 'muzika' was starting and there was to be dancing for the grown-ups from three o'clock in the afternoon until midnight.

Tomash had had a strenuous day, and although he was very happy, it was a relief to get out of the saddle.

29

"It feels good to have the ropes off my arms," he exclaimed to Yurka, who was gazing at him in wrapt admiration.

"Was it hard to hold the rose in your mouth for so long?"

"Not at all, but it was bumpy and uncertain to ride without holding on."

Starechek started to chuckle. "Are you complaining about such a gentle ride? Why, when I was a lad, a rival village would carry off the King, and then there would be a real battle between the two sides, with wild riding back and forth. I remember once, when I was King. . . ."

Marushka, Tomash and Yurka looked at their grandfather for a moment; dear little Starechek with his wrinkles and white, white hair. Was it possible? Was he ever that young? Did he ever ride swiftly? But they did not stop for answers to their questioning thoughts. The 'muzika' was in full swing and they were allowed to listen to the fun from across the street. That is, they could listen until six o'clock, and then they would go home without being told, have a bite to eat and go to bed by themselves.

Yurka did not like the idea of putting himself to bed, but if he ever expected to ride as a King, he would have to be like Tomash, and Tomash did not complain.

yarka Bures

Harvest

THE SUMMER was generous in its gifts. Ripening fields had
given promise of a rich harvest. Marushka, Tomash and Yurka
had grown two shades deeper in tan and their eyes sparkled
happily as they worked in the fields. The older children were a
real help in the field-work and although Yurka's work was
equally important, he felt that it was not enough for him to be
doing. He was tending neighbor Vavrova's new baby!

Neighbor Vavrova would bring the baby down to the field
each morning. She would stick two poles into the ground about
three feet apart. Then she would take a burlap square, in which
grass was ordinarily carried, and tie it to the poles. This made a
lovely hammock in which the baby slept away the best hours
of a beautiful day. It was fun at first, just watching the prepara-

3 1

tions, but as time went on and nothing very exciting ever happened, it became a little tiresome.

The field-work was hard and Marushka would be sent off to play whenever she looked tired. Yurka really appreciated that; it was always pleasant, because Marushka knew how to make dolls out of poppies. Yurka did not particularly like poppy-dolls, but they were better than a live doll that one could not touch, and certainly, ever so much better than nothing at all. So they made dolls. They pulled the petals off the picked poppy. The poppy-seed pod was the head with its tiny crown of hair. Then they slipped the petals back on the stem in the opposite way from which they grew. This made the skirt and they could change the skirts from pink to red, and then again to white by changing the petals.

At the end of the day, when they rode home in the wagon, Tatichek always let the children sit up in front with him, and this of course was great fun.

Before they knew it, the summer was nearly over. The wheat and rye had been cut and tied, and heaped in little mounds all over the field. Everyone was talking about the harvest-festival.

Tomash, Stepan and Yurka were tying streamers to the hay-wagon and harness. Yanko the blacksmith was helping them. "Anichka will be very beautiful in the 'Aldamash,' don't you think, Yanko?" It was odd that everybody liked to talk about Anichka when Yanko was near.

Yanko looked quickly at Tomash, but the boy pretended he had said nothing unusual, so Yanko quietly answered, "Yes."

"Oh, I forgot!" interrupted Yurka . . . and Yanko was grateful. . . . "I promised to help them make the Aldamash!" and off flew Yurka to the garden where Anichka, Marushka and two of the field-girls were making the wreath.

It was a strange wreath indeed; it could more correctly have

As time went on, it became tiresome

been called a bouquet. A huge bunch of field-flowers was the center or hub of the wheel, and long ribbons fell like a shower from its rim. Two ribbons were tied over its top, so that it could hang like a lantern.

Yurka had come too late, the Aldamash was finished. However, he was allowed to tie a gay red ribbon around a choice sheaf of wheat that Anichka, as queen of the harvest, was to carry. Even this little task was an honor, thought Yurka, so that he did not feel badly about the Aldamash.

At last everything was in readiness for the event of the afternoon and the Horak household had finished a hastily eaten dinner. To tell the truth, the children hardly ate anything at all, but Mamichka kindly overlooked it, realizing how excited they were.

The very special prayer which Yurka had said the night before, was indeed answered. The day was one of those rare August days, turquoise blue skies, golden sun and a gentle, gentle breeze that made the ribbons on the Aldamash flutter.

Yanko's heart fluttered too when he saw his dear Anichka sitting on the straw throne in the brightly decorated wagon. He could not see her sweet smile, for the Aldamash was perched on her head and the streamers hid her face, but he looked fondly at her fine, strong hands. They were clasped firmly about the sheaf of wheat tied with the red ribbon. How many kind and useful things those dear hands had done!

"Here we are!" They had driven out to the fields and back again to the Horaks. Stepan leaped down from his driver's seat and went to the gate to knock. The field-hands climbed down from the wagon and helped Anichka from her golden throne.

> *Housekeeper, fling wide your gate*
> *And do not think us bold.*
> *Hasten pray, don't hesitate;*
> *We bring a wreath of gold.*

34

They all sang so lustily, that Mamichka, Tatichek, and the Grandparents hurried out to greet the merrymakers. Mamichka stepped forward to accept, first, the sheaf of wheat, and then the Aldamash, which was taken off Anichka's head. She thanked the young people and asked them to take supper with the family. Then she carried the Aldamash into the living-room, where she hung it by its top ribbons over the table. It looked very much like a lovely chandelier.

All those who had helped the Horaks in the fields were there. It was a jolly group that sat at the festive supper-table, out in the courtyard. Once or twice Yurka grew so excited his voice was heard far above the others', but Tomash or Marushka reminded him each time that although they were a part of the party, it was not a children's party. Yurka understood what they meant and was more careful after that.

Uncle Skopek was there too. He had had some business to attend to in the village. In fact, that very day, he had sold a velvety-brown cow to Tatichek and was asked to stay on for the supper and dancing that night.

"And when you come to our house Sunday," he was telling Yurka, "you shall see at least six cows and a fine bull, and Fanka will take you to the village-green after Benediction, and there you'll ride the merry-go-round, and Fanka will buy you a big heart of ginger-bread. Or perhaps you'd prefer a horse and rider?" Uncle Skopek knew so many funny little stories, that Yurka listened in wrapt attention late into the night, while all the others danced and made merry.

The following Sunday, the Horak family was awake with the earliest bird, which meant four o'clock. It was the Feast-day of St. Mary. They were making a pilgrimage to the neighboring village where there was a beautiful shrine. Then, too, they were going to visit with the Skopeks, Mamichka's sister and brother-in-law, who lived in this same village. This would be a true holi-

The ginger-bread rider and horse

day, thought Marushka, because she adored her five cousins, four boys and a girl, and they in turn loved her very much.

It was only a short two hours' walk, and by seven o'clock the Horaks had reached the outskirts of the village. Petr, Pavel, Alesh and Voyta were there to meet them and were glad to greet their cousins, whom they had not seen for several months.

Little Voyta let out squeals of delight when Marushka handed him the wooden whistle she had brought for him. "Tatichek made it for you, Voyta. It really makes music, if you know just where to put your fingers to stop up the holes."

"It makes eight beautiful tones," added Tomash, "if you blow right." But Voyta was no longer listening; he was hurrying on ahead to tell his sister Fanka about his good luck.

This was a larger village than the one in which the Horaks lived, and the church was a great deal finer than theirs. It was set on a high hill, but it was not a hard climb up to it, because the slope was gentle. When they reached the top, Marushka looked back in the direction from which they had come. Up the winding road came a stream of people, all dressed in their Sunday best. Marushka looked to the left. Up another winding road came another stream of people, and as she turned right, she saw a hurrying crowd of worshippers. There were, in all, seven roads leading to the church from seven different villages, and the red kerchiefs on the women's heads made the roads look like seven streams of red poppies winding gently to the hill-top.

After church, there was a dinner of young goose, dumplings, cabbage, kolachky and many other goodies. Tetichka, that is, Auntie, was a splendid cook, as are most Czech and Slovak women, and everyone complimented her very much. Fanka, too, came in for her share of praise, for although she was only twelve, she had baked the kolachky herself, and they were so delicious, everyone had eaten two or three.

Fanka was a quiet child and preferred the company of Yurka to that of the other children. She was so calm and capable. Perhaps it was because she had four lively brothers, whom she was always mothering. It seemed she could scarcely remember the time when she was not leading a little brother by the hand, and so, when Yurka came to visit, it was only natural for her to take charge of him.

After Benediction, both families went directly to the village square. What fun it was to examine the wares laid out on each counter of the booths! These little stalls, put up specially for the occasion, were on all four sides of the square, and Marushka

37

thought they looked like a bright hem edging an enormous kerchief.

Yurka did not notice this, but his eyes sparkled as Fanka led him from one booth to the other, and together they tried to decide which was the prettier: the ginger-bread heart, or the rider and horse. The latter was chosen because the horse had a tempting pink sugar-icing tail.

Topping all the rest of the excitement were rides on the merry-go-round. There were cries of "Isn't it beautiful?" "See the fine black horse!" "May we ride again?" "It's like a fairy-story!"

It was not as fine a merry-go-round as city children are accustomed to riding, but to these children, used to only the simplest amusements, it was enchanting. The tail was missing from one pony, a leg from another, and the gilt was off in some spots and almost black in others, but none of these things mattered to the Horak or Skopek children.

"They'll stay on forever, if we let them," said Mamichka, and then suddenly she noticed that Yurka was turning a little green around the mouth. "Take them off, Tatichek, they've had enough. Look at Yurka's face!"

Yurka was sorry that he had spoiled the fun for the others, but Tatichek made things easier by saying, "It's really time for us to be on our way home, anyway. The two hours' walk back will stretch into three at the end of such a day, so the sooner we start, the better."

There was a cry of protest from all the Skopeks.

"What!" cried Auntie. "Go home? Why, we baked all day yesterday! There are buchty, kolachky, coffee and buttermilk. What will we do with all the food?"

"Fanka churned fresh butter for you," added Uncle Skopek. "Certainly, you can't disappoint Fanka!"

Of course they could not disappoint Fanka, so back they

The horse had a tempting pink sugar-icing tail

went to the Skopeks' fine white house and had another real feast! "You will need every bit of it, with the trip ahead of you," explained Auntie, as though they were going on an ocean voyage, and nothing could stop her from wrapping separate little parcels of food for each one of them to carry home.

Suddenly, just as the Horaks were about to leave, there was a sharp crack of a whip and up drove Tonda, Uncle Skopek's youngest brother, in the Skopeks' new wagon.

"Tonda will drive you home," announced Uncle, and nothing that the older Horaks could say in protest made any difference. They were all hustled into the wagon, and soon the two horses, black as crows, were making the long two-hour walk into a short one-hour drive.

Before long, Yurka was asleep, his head on Mamichka's lap, and he was dreaming that he was riding a ginger-bread horse with a pink tail, riding up and down as he did on the pony on the merry-go-round.

The Horak children slept happily that night

School Starts

"My, my!" cried Starenka as Yurka strutted into the sitting-room. Two salty little tears pushed themselves into the corners of her eyes. "What a man you are! . . . What fine trousers! . . . Turn around and let me see the back of you!"

Yurka proudly turned about to show off the back of his brand-new trousers. He did not suspect that Starenka had him turn so that she might wipe away the tears from her dear, soft cheeks. It would have worried him to see his beloved grandma cry; much more so, if he had thought it was his fault that she was crying!

One by one, the rest of the family stole into the room, and each one, in turn, stayed on to admire the new Yurka. They had all seen him in the long loose white trousers that little boys wear during the summer when they graze the geese, but these handsome new white pants that tucked into the boot-tops were indeed wonderful!

Yurka felt that he had grown at least four centimeters in just that one morning. It was too bad he had to go to school with Marushka and Tomash! It was so childish! But at any rate, it was better than having to be dragged to school by Mamichka's hand, as Mikesh was led last year! And Mikesh was crying and his mother complaining, which was the worst thing in the world. It made one look like such a baby!

Marushka stepped up to Mamichka and kissed her hand, then she turned to Tatichek and kissed his hand. Tomash followed her example, and then Yurka solemnly followed Tomash.

"Remember your manners, Yurka," reminded Marushka, "and when the teacher asks you a question, answer politely."

"And don't ask too many questions yourself, Yurka. It is by listening that one learns," added Tomash.

They entered the schoolhouse. It was not a very large building, but there were at least six rooms all on one floor. Yurka counted them. All the rooms were fitted out in much the same way, he noticed, the teacher's table and chair, long benches and desks for the children, who sat ten in a row, and a large blackboard.

Marushka and Tomash led Yurka to the beginners' room, and Yurka was glad they did. He was not quite as brave as he had expected to be.

"This is Horak, Mr. Schoolmaster," explained Marushka. "Horak, the younger: Yurka."

Yurka, with his hat in hand, bowed and said, "Praised be the Lord!" in his most grown-up tone, but his voice seemed very far away. The teacher patted him on the head and assured him that they would get along nicely together, if Yurka paid strict attention to his lessons.

Yurka regained his confidence. "I have already promised Starenka that I would read to her next Sunday." The schoolmaster smiled knowingly at the two older children, and Marushka and Tomash felt old beyond their years.

It seems, however, that for each kindly, smiling schoolmaster in this particular school, there had to be one cross one, and

43

Yurka goes to school

Tomash was entering the class of just such an irritable one. Perhaps the Headmaster thought this was the type best suited to teach boys of eleven and twelve.

Schoolmaster Patek never smiled, and seemed to even dislike seeing anyone else do so. He had worn a sour expression for so long that his face was all creased and wrinkled, like an old crinkled pocket-handkerchief. All the other teachers kept their reed whips on their desks. Not so Schoolmaster Patek. He always had one in his hand, ever ready to mete out punishment. Whether or not it was due, it seemed that if his whip did not see action every fifteen minutes, the big blue veins at his temples would burst with fury!

The grumpy master had been called out of the room by the Headmaster and there was very little, in fact, nothing, the boys could do to occupy themselves. After all, it was the first day of school!

"Psssst!" hissed Karel to Tomash, who sat ahead of him. "This is stupid! To just sit so!" And soon there was a growing restlessness that finally loosened the valve for the stored-up energy of the morning.

"He's not coming back; let's play beans!"

"Who has them?"

"I do."

"You can't play it, you've got boots on."

"Vanya's barefoot; let him shoot."

So it was decided. Vanya would shoot.

He stood very tall and straight, the other boys closely grouped about him. Most of the boys had dried beans in their pockets, which they carried for this favorite game. Looking down at his toe, Vanya held the bean up to his eye with the air of an expert. He aimed carefully, and let the bean drop. If it missed Vanya's brown toe, the boy got back his bean; if the bean hit the goal, Vanya kept it.

The game was getting more and more exciting. Vanya had missed his toe only a very few times and his pockets were bulging, that is, those that were not full of holes. Quite suddenly there was a sharp swish and Tomash let out a piercing scream.

"So, this is how you study when I leave the room for a moment!" and another swish caught the back of a second boy, who had been watching the game at much closer range, having bent himself double over the desk in front of him.

"It wouldn't have been so bad, although he whips awfully hard," said Tomash, as he and his sister and brother were walking home at noon, "but after he thrashed us all, he gave Vanya an extra ten lashings and then took all the beans away from him, and most of the time, that's all Vanya and his mother have to eat . . . those beans that he wins from us."

"I like Vanya," Yurka declared. "He's always kind, and he works hard to help his mother, and he can't have boots—not even to go to church."

"It must be very cold to go barefoot in the Fall." Marushka shivered the least bit, thinking of the biting days of Autumn and Winter last year, when Vanya's toes looked so cold and blue that she had wanted to take off her own boots and let him have them.

By the next day, the story of the beans had spread through the school. That afternoon, Vanya carried beans home not only in his pockets, but he had two boots full of them, and the boots were large and strong enough to last him for five or six years.

The Horak children slept happily that night.

Saint Nicholas

I AM A GOOD BOY
I AM A GOOD BOY
I AM A GOOD BOY

"What is that you are writing, Yurka? May I see?" Yurka screwed up his tiny nose, that as yet had acquired no definite shape, and studied the large sheet of white paper.

"I am writing to Saint Nicholas, to let him know how I've

behaved, and when he comes tomorrow night, I shall hand it to him. Is it written well?"

Marushka, who was already in her second year at school and therefore felt very wise, eyed the printed words critically. She was proud that Yurka had learned so much in such a short while in school and did not hesitate to tell him so. "However," she added, "I think I should not write that sentence any more. The good saint may suspect that you are trying to hide something from him, with so much writing. Just sign your name."

"And you might sign mine too, because I'll not have time to write him a report this year," suggested Tomash, who was at the other end of the table, drawing colorful designs on a small wooden chest.

"For shame, Tomash!" cried Marushka. "Too lazy to write for yourself. I hope Saint Nicholas did not hear you!" and she pricked her finger with the embroidery needle. "That's what I get," she said to herself, "for scolding my own brother!"

Yurka signed his name. The letters of his name were twice as large as those in the sentences, although he had not meant them to be.

"Shall I put an ornament in the corner?" he asked.

"It would be very nice," answered Marushka.

"What shall it be?"

The question interested even Tomash, and all three thought for a long while. Suddenly the older brother spoke up. "As long as Saint Nicholas brings us fruit and nuts, why not make *the little apple* design?"

That was an excellent idea, the other two children agreed, and Yurka started immediately to make the first design a Moravian child learns to draw, *The Little Apple*. When he had finished, it looked very fine indeed, just like a real apple cut in half. One could see the core, the seed-vessels and seeds, the stem at the bottom, and the bit of flower at the top. The colors

48

Have you been good Tomash?

Yurka used were not exactly natural, as it was painted in blue and yellow, as well as red, green and black. But no one would have any trouble at all recognizing *The Little Apple*.

The letter and drawing completed, Yurka folded it neatly and sighed. He had performed a delicate task with great dignity and he was satisfied that it was well done. Marushka and Tomash were too busy to pay much heed to what he was doing. Marushka was engrossed with the last row of cross-stitching on the linen square that she was making for Mamichka for Christmas, while Tomash was putting tiny black dots in the center of an ornament that he had made, and black dots needed one's undivided attention.

Yurka studied the room carefully. Where would the letter

find the safest resting place until Saint Nicholas came? He considered the wardrobe. No, they had too many clothes hung in it and the letter would be too easily swept out. The cupboard? His almost tragic experience with the powder in the cupboard made him suspicious of that hiding-place.

Ah! At last he had it! The stove, the baking-oven of the stove. It opened into the hallway, and no one would see him put it there, providing he made no noise. Today was Thursday. There would be no baking until Saturday, and tomorrow, just before Saint Nicholas would come, Yurka could get his precious letter. Yurka tip-toed out into the hall-way to the oven door, quietly opened it, and slipped the beautiful paper into the opening.

Early the next morning Yurka was awakened by a most pleasant smell, the smell of baking bread. Anichka had been up and about for hours, and since there was so much to do before Sunday, she decided to do her baking today. Today! Why today was Saint Nicholas Eve! Saint Nicholas Eve! Anichka baking in the baking-oven! The baking-oven, where he had put his beautiful letter that was to say so much for him!

"Anichka! Anichka! You've burned it! He won't see it! He won't see it!" Poor little Yurka was beside himself!

Kind Anichka tried hard to rescue the treasured letter, as soon as she was able to understand Yurka's frantic cries, but it was too late. The large sheet of white paper had turned the golden brown of a well-baked loaf of bread!

"Don't cry, Yurka! I'm very sorry. But I wouldn't worry too much, if I were you. After all, Saint Nicholas and his Angel may have been here during the night to see whether the chimney was clean enough for them to come through. Perhaps they had already read your letter!"

Yurka blinked away his tears. Perhaps this was true. Mamichka had told him that Saint Nicholas comes through the chimney, though she had never actually seen him do so. Besides, to be cross on the very day he was expected might bring a black mark against Yurka's name on the record. So he decided not to cry.

It seemed the day would never turn into dark night, but at last, supper was over and the children sat down at the table, each one trying hard to do his work. Marushka had put away her finished linen square, but she was busily knitting a stocking. Mamichka was teaching her how to turn the heel but Marushka was paying more attention to the door than to her mother. Yurka was trying to carve a funny wooden doll for Vavrova's baby and Tomash was busy reading a story-book.

Knock! Knock! Yurka's heart skipped a beat. So did Marushka's. Tomash could not quite make up his mind whether to be excited or not. Tap, tap, tap. That was Saint Nicholas' staff. Rattle, rattle, rattle. That was the Devil's chain, and in walked the three—Saint Nicholas, tall and splendid looking in his bishop's robe and mitre and flowing white beard; the Angel in white draperies that were studded with stars, and finally the Devil himself, in a black suit that made him look like a chimney-sweep. The Devil's face was as red and ugly as the Angel's was white and beautiful.

Saint Nicholas wasted no time. "I have many other places to go tonight," he explained. Although the children had been told to say their prayers as soon as the saint appeared, and prayers were to be said with downcast eyes, Tomash could not help stealing a glance at the Good One. . . . His voice sounded so much like the blacksmith, Yanko's, even though the sound was muffled by the long beard.

"Have you been good, Tomash?" Tomash was so startled out of his doubts by the thunderous question, he began to stutter, "I . . . I . . . I have tried."

"Indeed he has tried," and Mamichka's voice spoke reassuringly. Tomash was grateful to her.

"Put it in the book. And what would you like for Christmas?" asked Saint Nicholas.

Saint Nicholas

"I should like a violin, if that's not asking too much."

"We shall see, we shall see. Put it in the book." And the Angel took great pains to write down everything carefully.

"And you, Marushka? What would you like?"

Marushka turned quite red and for all the promises she had made to herself that *this* year she would look Saint Nicholas in the eye, she found that her lids were to heavy to raise.

"Speak up, Marushka," urged her mother. "Saint Nicholas must be on his way. What would you like most of all?"

"I'd like . . . most of all . . . I'd like a baby sister!"

"Put it down, put it down." And the Angel wrote very quickly. "And if there are no baby sisters this year, there may be a doll that will look just like one."

Yurka was very hot one moment, and very cold the next. The Devil had a terrible way of rattling the chain and looking right at him. Yurka's tongue just simply stuck to the roof of his mouth!

"Well, well, this is the good boy, Yurka. This is the good boy who wrote me the long letter. You have his name, do you not, my good Angel?" and Saint Nicholas looked at the record-book, "to make certain that the name was spelled correctly," he explained. Then he added, "What is it you want? Is it a horse? . . . A black horse like Yanko's?"

"That would be too big for Yurka," explained Mamichka. "Perhaps a smaller one, a black rocking-horse would be better, good Saint," and Yurka nodded his approval.

"And now that you have been such well-behaved children, you may have these apples and nuts from our bag. Put them on the table, Devil! The Angel will carry his book up to Heaven to the Christ-child, and there the Child will read the records. Then, on Christmas Eve, He will come to you and bring His gifts to you in memory of the gifts that were brought to Him long, long ago." And before anyone could move, Saint Nicholas was gone, gone for another year.

A Child Is Born

A Child Is Born

IT WAS so strange to be walking across the white snow, so very late at night, thought Marushka. An atmosphere of mystery and deep reverence seemed blended in the air. It was Christmas Eve, and everything was very, very still, everything except the crunch of the crisp snow, beneath the feet of those on their way to church.

What a day it had been! A day full of happenings! For the first time in his life, Yurka was able to fast until supper-time!

"You shall see the Golden Pig," Mamichka had promised, "if you can manage not to eat a bite of anything until supper!"

Much to everyone's surprise, Yurka did hold out, and so he saw the Golden Pig race across the sitting-room, just as he sat, drawing in his book. Tomash was the only one of the three Horak children who had grown wise to the fact that Anichka flashed a mirror on the wall to make the Pig, but he was kind enough not to spoil the fun of the others by saying anything about it.

The other events of the day danced across Marushka's mind —sitting down to a delicious supper of mushroom soup, fish and black gravy with prunes, dumplings; and last, but most important, cooked farina flavored with honey, butter and ginger.

Marushka remembered that this last food was exactly what the shepherds brought the little Christ Child as He lay in the manger. Then, scraps of the food and wafers were carried out to the animals in the stable. After that, the family gathered around a Christmas tree. It was gaily decorated with candies, fruits, and tiny candles. Here the gifts were distributed. A violin for Tomash, the rocking-horse for Yurka, and the doll for Marushka were all there. And Marushka recalled that Mamichka and the rest of the grown-ups were so grateful for *their* gifts.

"Weren't the wire-workers kind to come to our door to sing tonight," said Marushka, breaking the silence.

"To be sure they were," Mamichka agreed. She knew why the little boys from Slovakia came to the Horak door each year, singing carols as they carried the little wood-carvings of the Nativity. Tatichek never turned them away. A good meal and the night's lodging was their reward each Christmas Eve.

Marushka was in deep thought again. It was queer! Anichka had grown so red when after everyone had thrown one boot each, over his head, Anichka's boot pointed out, and Mamichka had laughingly said that surely Anichka would be the first to leave home. Tatichek had added, "Perhaps to get married!" Marushka hoped Anichka would not get married too soon! Suddenly, in the midst of the fun, had come the trumpet call, announcing High Midnight Mass, and now, here they were, trudging through the deep snow on their way to church.

"Oh, Anichka, you won't get married right away, will you?" whispered Marushka, as they neared the church.

"Hush, child!" admonished Anichka, "we mustn't speak of those things now. This is the Child's night and we must think of nothing but Him."

They were inside the church now, and soon the choir was singing. Tomash's voice could be heard above all the others in the choir as they sang the beautiful old Czech carols. The old organ, which was ordinarily very wheezy, took on a new and heavenly quality as it blended with the orchestra of village musicians.

Just before the close of Mass, fourteen shepherds from six different villages walked down the center-aisle, carrying lighted candles. They were dressed in their simple shepherd cloaks, but they moved with great dignity, as they neared the altar. Down the side aisles they went to the door of the church, where they each took a long thin shepherd's horn, and moving up the center aisle again, stood, each at his station. All at once, as though they had rehearsed for weeks, they raised the horns to their lips and blew a long blast that could be heard for kilometers about.

"Where are they going now?" whispered Yurka, as the shepherds filed out of the church.

"Home," replied Tatichek.

"But one of them is Uncle Skopek's man. Will he go home too?"

"Of course he will," was Tatichek's answer.

"Isn't it far to walk?" queried Yurka anxiously.

"The shepherds walked much farther than that to see the Babe, and kneel at His feet."

By this time the Horak family had reached the door of the church. "See," said Tatichek, "each shepherd has a lantern and is on his way home."

Marushka watched the lights of the shepherds, until they looked like tiny Saint-John-flies, twinkling in the distance. Then she looked up into the sky, and seeing one star that shone brighter than the rest in the darkness above, murmured gently to herself, "Do you suppose that could be the same Star that led the shepherds before?"

A New Horizon

"IF THOSE are your plans," Tatichek was saying, "we would never think of standing in your way." He was talking very quietly to Yanko, the young blacksmith who liked Anichka so much. "Mamichka, Yanko has something to say to you too."

Mamichka hurried in from the kitchen, where she was making fried cakes for this last day before Lent. There had been so many holidays since Christmas, she had hardly taken a breathing-spell. In fact, she was just a tiny bit glad that Lent and quiet were almost here!

"What is it, Yanko?" asked her low sweet voice.

Yanko seemed to gain courage. He blushed a deep, deep red, but this time did not lose his tongue. "You know I love Anichka," he said simply.

"I've known it for a long, long time."

"You have been almost a mother to her, and I am grateful to you."

"It has not been hard to be good to Anichka," was Mamichka's reply.

"I do not doubt it. I have come to you as she has no mother or father . . . to ask for her hand. I want to marry her."

"You are a kind man, Yanko. You may have her with our blessing. Is it not so, Tatichek?"

"Of course, of course!" heartily agreed Tatichek.

"Even if I want to take her to America?" asked Yanko anxiously.

"America!" exclaimed Mamichka.

"America?" "America?" "America?" cried three other voices from the corner, and up popped Tomash, Marushka, and Yurka, who were supposed to be doing their lessons at the table and not to be listening to what was going on around them. Tatichek and Mamichka were not angry at the children, however, but turned

Anichka

to Yanko again. Yanko was fine and strong. He would always be kind to Anichka, no matter how far away they were from home.

"You will take good care of Anichka, I am sure, Yanko," and Mamichka's voice trembled, so that Yurka was afraid she was going to cry.

"That I promise!" Yanko cried earnestly.

"America will be glad to have you for a new son and daughter. She welcomes such courageous people as you. Surely a country is happy that can benefit by gifts of such strength of character, the gifts of many nations of the world—to mould into one fine nation within its embrace. Tomash, call in Anichka."

Tomash rushed into the kitchen, where Anichka was pretending to be the busiest person in the world. Actually, everything seemed to be dropping from her fingers at that very moment.

"Anichka! Anichka!" cried Tomash breathlessly. "You're going to America!"

Anichka did not seem at all surprised! That was funny, thought Tomash.

"You're to come into the sitting-room this minute! Tatichek and Mamichka want you." He thought he wouldn't say anything about Yanko.

Anichka took off her apron and smoothed her hair with an unsteady hand. As she turned towards Tomash, he saw that her eyes were full of tears. Why did every one want to cry. The boy took Anichka's hand in his. "Don't cry, Anichka. This should be a very happy day for you."

"It is, Tomash. But you know, sometimes we cry, even on our days of joy."

There was a lump in Tomash's throat as he squeezed her hand, "Yes, I understand," was all he could say.

Marushka and Yurka rushed up to Anichka as she entered the sitting-room and threw their arms about her, crying, "Anichka,

Anichka, you're going to America! Isn't it wonderful? Across the ocean! Where there are Indians!"

"Hush, Yurka! . . . Where did you get that? . . . America is not full of Indians! Where did you hear such a thing? What an idea!" and Tatichek, who had read a great deal about America, explained how beautiful and livable America had become in a very short while, and what glorious promise the New World offered young people who were willing to work hard and honestly. "But step aside now, while I ask the blessing of the Lord on these dear ones of ours."

The children stepped aside obediently, as Anichka, the hired girl, and Yanko, the blacksmith, knelt before Tatichek and Mamichka. Tatichek put his hands on the heads of the kneeling couple and raising his eyes, prayed that they might be shown the righteous path and bring to their chosen home, America, loyalty, honesty, and faith.

Then everyone wept a little, until Yurka's voice piped, "When I grow up to be a man, I am coming to America to see you."

"Indeed you will!" answered Yanko heartily.

"And I will too!" asserted Tomash.

"Of course you will!" Yanko assured him.

"Do you suppose a girl might come, too?" ventured Marushka, timidly.

Anichka gathered the little girl into her arms, crying, "Dear little Marushka, of course you may, of course you may!"

Suddenly, from the corner where the grandparents were sitting unnoticed, there came a thin, thready voice singing:

> *Parting, ah, parting drear!*
> *Parting from those so dear!*
> *Drying eyes with snow-white kerchief,*
> *Drying eyes with snow-white kerchief;*
> *Wiping away each tear!*

That night Anichka was unusually gentle as she tucked the children into their fluffy beds. When Anichka left the room to return to the sitting-room where plans for the wedding and departure for America were being discussed, Marushka sighed deeply.

"What's the matter, Marushka?" asked Tomash.

"I can't sleep," answered Marushka. "Think of it! America! Do you truly expect that we shall see it one day?"

"I will, I know!" declared Tomash.

"Me too!" echoed Yurka . . . "and I'll find those Indians . . . and horses . . . and boats . . . and . . ." Slowly his voice trailed off . . .

"I'd like the big oceans that are on both sides . . . and the tall buildings, . . . wide rivers, . . . and big trees . . ." and Tomash dropped off . . .

"I'd like them too, . . . so beautiful, . . . so free, . . . everything . . . if Mamichka and Tatichek . . . could . . . be . . . there . . . too . . ." and Marushka's beautiful brown eyes were closed in sleep.